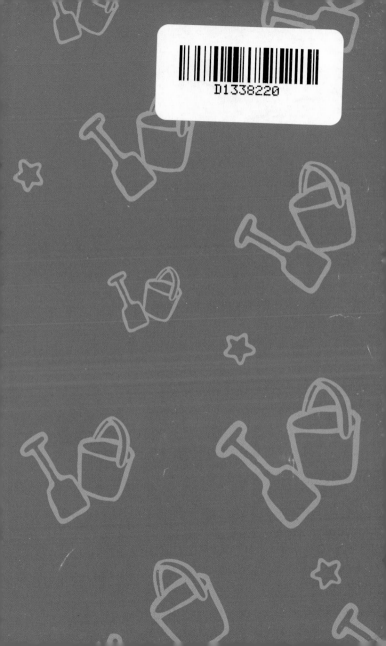

D1338220

EGMONT

We bring stories to life

This edition first published in 2010 by Dean,
an imprint of Egmont UK Limited,
239 Kensington High Street, London, W8 6SA

Postman Pat® © 2010 Woodland Animations Ltd,
a division of Classic Media UK Limited.
Licensed by Classic Media Distribution Limited.
Original writer John Cunliffe.
From the original television design by Ivor Wood.
Royal Mail and Post Office imagery is used by kind
permission of Royal Mail Group plc.

ISBN 978 0 6035 6520 5
3 5 7 9 10 8 6 4 2
Printed and bound in Italy

Postman Pat
at the Seaside

EGMONT

It was a very sunny day in Greendale. Jess was lazily sunbathing on the bonnet of Postman Pat's van.

"Phew, it's hot!" said Pat. "Come on, Jess. We've got two bags of post to deliver!"

Postman Pat's first stop was the station café. He had a postcard for Meera.

"It's from cousin Sanjay!" cried Meera. "He's at the seaside! Can we go to the seaside too, Mum?"

"It's too far to go just for the day, Meera," replied Meera's mum, Nisha.

"Well, I'm sure you'll find something else to do!" smiled Pat.

While Postman Pat was in the café,
Ted Glen was getting into a real pickle.
He had driven over a bump in the road
and all of the sand had tipped out of
his truck! "Oh 'eck!" he groaned.

PC Selby was scooping up the sand with his helmet when Postman Pat appeared.

"It can't stay here, Ted," PC Selby muttered. "It makes the place look untidy."

"The question is, how are we going to move it?" asked Ted.

"Well, you won't move much sand like that!" chuckled Pat. "Tell you what, let's use these spare mailbags."

They started filling the
mailbags with sand,
but it fell out of holes
in the bags.

"Oh dear, that's just no
good at all," grumbled Pat. Then he caught
sight of Reverend Timms pushing his
wheelbarrow across the churchyard.
"Hmm, I've got an idea," thought Pat.

Meanwhile, Ajay had also had an idea – a family picnic. The Bains' set off for Thompson Ground.

"Here we are!" smiled Ajay.
"The perfect spot for a sunny picnic!"

Just then they heard a loud buzzing sound
behind them.

"Er, Dad, what's that noise?" asked Meera,
looking around.

"It's getting louder!" said Nisha.

Suddenly a mysterious veiled figure
appeared from behind the hedge.
It was Dorothy Thompson, dressed
in her beekeeper's clothing.

the phone to his friends.

Charlie. You tell Tom and
call Lucy. See you there –
et your bucket and spade!"

"I'm afraid you can't have your picnic
here," she told them. "Didn't you see the
beehives? We're building a proper stand
for them, when Ted gets here with the
sand. Why don't you go up to Greendale
Farm instead?"

On the village Green, Pat and Ted were in a spot of bother. They had filled the vicar's wheelbarrow with sand – and then the wheel had fallen off!

"Oh, crumbs! What will we do now, Pat?" said Ted, worriedly.

"Aha!" said Pat. "I hear a vacuum cleaner. I wonder . . ."

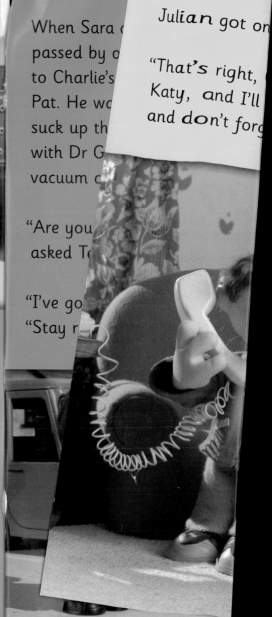

When Sara … passed by o… to Charlie's … Pat. He w… suck up th… with Dr G… vacuum c…

"Are you… asked T…

"I've go… "Stay r…

Julian got on

"That's right, Katy, and I'll and don't forg…

Meanwhile the Bains' had arrived at
Greendale Farm, and their picnic was
all ready.

"At last!" sighed Meera, sitting down.

"That walking has made me hungry!"
said Ajay. "Let's eat!"

Ajay was just about to bite into his
sandwich, when . . .

Baaa! A flock of sheep came to join
their picnic!

"Go away! Shoo!" shouted Ajay, but the
sheep wouldn't budge.

"It's no good, Ajay," said Nisha. "We'll have
to go somewhere else."

They trudged up to the
top of Greendale Hill.

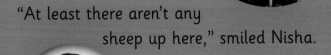

"Phew, it's steep,"
puffed Meera.

"At least there aren't any
sheep up here," smiled Nisha.

"Or bees!" joked Meera.

But soon there was no picnic
either! When Ajay
took off his backpack,
it rolled down the
hill, spilling their
food as
it went.

"I give up!"
groaned Ajay.

Back in Greendale, everyone watched anxiously as the vacuum cleaner got fuller and fuller . . . and fuller and then . . . BOOM! The bag burst, showering them all with sand.

"Oh dear!" said PC Selby. "Looks like we'll have to use our hats after all!"

But Julian and his friends had other plans!
They arrived with their buckets and spades.

"I've brought some friends to play, Dad.
Right everyone, get digging!"

"But Julian . . . wait!" gasped Pat.

"This is like being
at the seaside,"
laughed Charlie.

"Now that gives
me the best idea
yet!" grinned Pat.
"Gather round,
everyone!"

With help from everyone and in no time at all, Ted Glen's sand was spread across the Green. Deckchairs and umbrellas were

placed around a paddling pool and
a volleyball net had been put up.
It looked just like the seaside!

Making their way back home from their
disastrous picnic, the Bains' were amazed
when they reached the village Green.

"What on earth?" said Ajay.

"Wow!" gasped Meera.

"Well," chuckled Pat. "If the Bains' can't get to the seaside, the seaside must come to the Bains'!"

And everyone had a wonderful, sunny afternoon at Greendale-on-sea!

When Sara and Julian
passed by on their way
to Charlie's, they saw
Pat. He was about to
suck up the sand
with Dr Gilbertson's
vacuum cleaner!

"Are you sure it'll work, Pat?"
asked Ted doubtfully.

"I've got a better idea, Dad," called Julian.
"Stay right there!"

Julian got on the phone to his friends.

"That's right, Charlie. You tell Tom and Katy, and I'll call Lucy. See you there – and don't forget your bucket and spade!"